Where's Pup?

by Dayle Ann Dodds

pictures by Pierre Pratt

Tundra Books

Published in Canada by Tundra Books,
481 University Avenue, Toronto, Ontario M5G 2E9

Published in the United States by Dial Books for Young Readers,
A division of Penguin Putnam Inc., 345 Hudson Street, New York, New York 10014

National Library of Canada Cataloguing in Publication Data

Dodds, Dayle Ann
     Where's pup? / Dayle Ann Dodds ; illustrated by Pierre Pratt.

ISBN 0-88776-622-6

I. Pratt, Pierre II. Title.
PZ7.D66Wh 2003   j813'.54   C2002-902576-1

We acknowledge the support of the Canada Council for the Arts and the Ontario Arts
Council for our publishing program. We acknowledge the financial support of the
Government of Canada through the Book Publishing Industry Development Program
for our publishing activities.

Design by Lily Malcom. Text set in Beton.
The art was painted using acrylic paints.
Printed in Hong Kong on acid-free paper.

1 2 3 4 5 6   08 07 06 05 04 03

To Dana, Katherine, and Grace
—D.D.

Where's Pup?

Don't know.
Go ask Jo.
She's feeding Mo.

Hello, Jo!
Hello, Mo!
Where's Pup?

Can't say.
Go ask Ray.
He's washing Kay.

Good day, Ray!
Good day, Kay!
Where's Pup?

No guess.

Go ask Jess.

He's training Bess.

Hi there, Jess!
Hi there, Bess!
Where's Pup?

Can't see.
Go ask Lee.
He's launching Dee.

Howdy, Lee!
Howdy, Dee!
Where's Pup?

No clue.
Go ask Sue.
She's riding Blue.

Hiya, Sue! Hiya, Blue!
Where's Pup?

Not here or there.
Go ask Claire.
She's catching Pierre.

Can't chat.
Go see Nat.
He's on the mat.

I see Nat
on the mat.
Can't find Pup.
I give up!